S0-BHS-038

MONSTERS, MIND YOUR MANNERS!

ELIZABETH SPURR Illustrations by SIMON SCALES

www.av2books.com

Go to **www.av2books.com**, and enter this book's unique code.

BOOK CODE

F215603

AV² by Weigl brings you media enhanced books that support active learning.

First Published by

Your AV² Media Enhanced book gives you a fiction readalong online. Log on to www.av2books.com and enter the unique book code from this page to use your readalong.

AV² Readalong Navigation

Published by AV² by Weigl
350 5th Avenue, 59th Floor New York, NY 10118

Printed in the United States of America in North Mankato, Minnesota
1 2 3 4 5 6 7 8 9 0 16 15 14 13 12

Published in 2011 by Albert Whitman & Company.

052012
WEP160512

Library of Congress Cataloging-in-Publication Data

Spurr, Elizabeth.
Monsters, mind your manners! / Elizabeth Spurr ; illustrations by Simon Scales.
p. cm.
Summary: Illustrations and rhyming text reveal the terrible ways monsters may behave in one's home, on crowded sidewalks, on a bus, or at school as they do what they wish without thinking of others.
ISBN 978-1-61913-124-8 (hardcover : alk. paper)
[1. Stories in rhyme. 2. Behavior--Fiction. 3. Etiquette--Fiction. 4. Monsters--Fiction. 5. Humorous stories.] I. Scales, Simon, ill. II. Title.
PZ8.3.S772Mon 2012
[E]--dc23 2012021485

Look out, children,
here they come,
bringing pandemonium!

Lock doors and windows, run and hide.
Do not let these creeps inside!

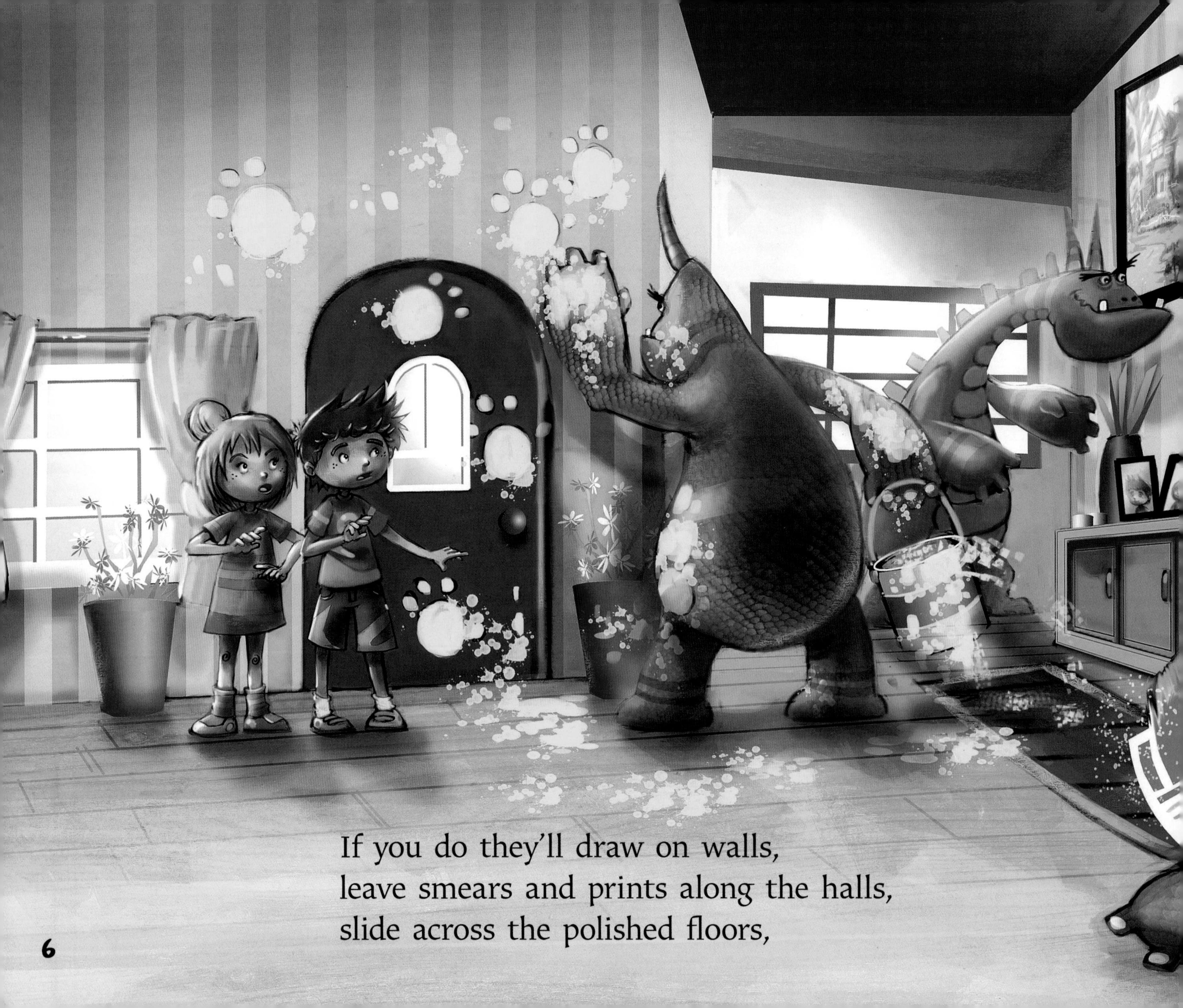

If you do they'll draw on walls,
leave smears and prints along the halls,
slide across the polished floors,

#1

start a baseball game indoors!

Those nervy MONSTERS
come in flocks
to bike and skate on
crowded walks.

They never think to move aside
until it's safe for them to ride.

MONSTERS love to shout and fuss
when riding on a crowded bus.
Rarely will they share a seat.
(They need that place to put their feet.)

MONSTERS always think it's cool
to talk and giggle when in school.

They snap their gum, or blow a bubble.
And think it's fun to get in trouble.

With mouths wide open, MONSTERS chew.
Yuck! Who wants to see that goo!

MONSTERS do not know it's rude
to start a battle with their food.

This one plays marbles
with his peas,
and never says "Thank you"
or "please."

When eating soup,
MONSTERS slurp.
And when they're finished,
loudly b-u-r-r-p!

MONSTERS despise tidiness.
They've made this room a
ghastly mess!

They pull the bath towels
off the rack,
but never think to hang
them back.

At bedtime MONSTERS always think
they need to pee, they need a drink.
They'll put up every kind of fight
to stay awake, keep on the light.

Too bad they never get to bed . . .

that's when the world's best books are read!